# Thief of Mar

Henry Hasse

**Alpha Editions**

This edition published in 2023

ISBN : 9789357941136

Design and Setting By
**Alpha Editions**
www.alphaedis.com
Email - info@alphaedis.com

# THIEF OF MARS

## BY HENRY HASSE

**Fate dealt Ron Jordan grim alternatives ... death by decree of the Space Patrol, or murder at the hands of this ruthless Martian pirate.**

Ron Jordan presented a disgusting sight of an Earthman in the last stages of dissipation, as he slouched along the single dark street of Halo City, the sardonically named pirate base on Ceres, Ron's clothing was dirty and worn, his shoulders hunched carelessly and his arms dangled by his side. A week's growth of beard was on his face, and his hair was ragged and unkempt. If he had straightened from his slouch he would have been an inch over six feet, with a lithe bulk that belied the height; and despite his unsavory appearance at the present moment, his gray eyes in the dark face were startlingly clear.

The outward appearance was all a disguise, for Jordan had a mission here.

From the crude stone buildings on either side of the street came sounds of drunken laughter, the click of gambling wheels, and occasional curses as some player lost. And once Jordan saw the thin, blue flash of an electric pistol. He shrugged, knowing that life was cheap among these cut-throat pirates of many planets; he'd seen more than a score of men die in the single month he'd been here.

As he neared the end of the street, one of the doors near him opened and two men staggered out. One was a bulking Martian with dark, leathery face and heavy-lidded eyes. The other was an Earthman. The Martian, a little drunk, stumbled into Jordan and cursed. Jordan mumbled an apology and tried to move unobtrusively out of the way. At this, the Martian's lips curved. He turned to his champion and said contemptuously:

"Listen to him. He apologizes. The scum!" With that word, he struck Jordan hard across the face with the back of his hand.

Jordan took the blow, falling to the street and cringing. Hot anger flooded his brain at the insult, and his muscles quivered. However, he restrained himself, for he had long ago decided that his mission here could only be accomplished passively. He peered up through eyes that were dull now, and saw the Martian's hand slide to the pistol in his belt. Jordan tensed, ready to launch himself up.

But the Martian's companion stopped him when his hand was on the pistol. "Don't waste a charge on him. Besides he's useful to us around here—runs errands, cleans out the ships, etc. I think he's a little touched." He tapped his head significantly, looking pityingly down at Jordan.

Jordan peered up and allowed his lips to part in an idiotic grin, revealing teeth and gums that were purplish as though from chewing the mind-destroying *Eishn* stems.

"You're right," the Martian said cruelly, "he's an *Eishn* hound. People who chew that stuff ought to live. Killing them'd be too merciful." He kicked Jordan in the ribs, and Jordan took that blow, too, clenching his teeth tight together. It would not do to make a stand yet.

He watched the two men move away, and then rose to his feet. It had been the smartest and safest thing he had done, never to have a pistol on him. No one was foolish enough to come to this pirate base unarmed, therefore they all looked upon him as "touched" and harmless. And he couldn't afford to get into any brawls—yet.

---

Jordan reached the great hollow space at the end of the street. This served as a spaceport, with ships of all sizes and designs resting there in scattered profusion. Pirates came here whenever they pleased, set down for a day or a week, and then left for places unknown and unasked. The entire hollow was pretty well concealed between ragged black cliffs that sheered up sharply on both sides.

Now Jordan moved out among the ships, searching for the one he had heard had just arrived that morning. Thus he had searched in the month he had been here, taking a careful look at each new arrival. He was waiting for *one* ship only, knowing it would be only a matter of time until it set down here. He would wait six months, a year, if necessary, until the *Lucifer* came. And when it did.... Jordan's lips pressed into a tight little line, as his eyes became space-cold and vengeful.

Ron Jordan was here to clear his brother, Carl, who had been sentenced to the Venus prison-swamp for life on a charge of smuggling Silicytes.[1] That was only a few months ago, and it was a false charge. Carl Jordan, stranded on Mars, had hired out to the *Lucifer*, a freighter purportedly scheduled for Earth. Instead, it had headed out toward Jupiter. It was the age-old shanghai trick. Four others besides Carl Jordan had been similarly duped. The owner and captain, a Martian named Tarnuff, explained that they'd be well paid upon reaching Callisto; and the men agreed, including Jordan. Then, reaching the asteroids, the ship set down on one of the large rocks and Tarnuff explained that they were to take on a cargo of Silicytes. The men, a villainous bunch anyway, still agreed—all except Jordan, who rebelled.

The men found a colony of Silicytes and were herding them into the ship when a Patrol ship was sighted sweeping upon them. Tarnuff, in return for Jordan's rebellion, knocked him out and left him on the asteroid. The Patrol ship pursued the *Lucifer* but lost it; then returned and found Carl Jordan there with the Silicytes. He had protested his innocence in vain, but in view of the circumstances he was only given a life sentence instead of the usual swift death penalty.

Now Ron Jordan peered around the hollow of the Ceres spaceport. More than a score of ships rested there. It was very dark but he recognized most of them. Then, on the far side, he saw it.

As he approached, and made out the design of the ship, his heart leaped. It might ... it just possibly might be the one! It was a Martian freighter all right, although rather sleek and slim with a suggestion of speed. He came nearer. There were the side tubes, four of them horizontally one above the other, unusually far forward, just as Carl had described! Ron moved to the rear of the ship. Yes! There were the triple rear tubes, flexible, resting along the wide fin which could raise or lower them; they were huge, six feet in diameter, with smaller auxiliary tubes arranged circularly around them. Ron's heart was pounding now. If this wasn't the *Lucifer*, it must be a twin! It was a solid black ship perfectly in keeping with the name.

He walked toward the prow, looking up at the circular ports as he passed; all were dark, apparently no one being aboard at present. He reached the prow, looked up for the name and saw it, dimly: *Martian Belle*. Ron's heart fell in his abrupt disappointment. Wrong, after all. It meant more weeks, perhaps months, of waiting, while his brother languished in the black Venus prison-swamp without news.

Ron started to walk away, when an idea occurred to him. He drew out a tiny torch, the only object he carried on him. It might be dangerous flashing a light around a strange ship, but he had to chance it. This ship was so very similar, that he had to be sure.

He clicked the penetro-button and flashed the powerful beam upward, playing it across the words *Martian Belle*. Then his heart leaped. A great square patch had been newly painted there! And beneath that patch his beam picked out the old letters: L-U-C-I-F-E-R.

Without wasting another second Jordan hurried to the dark cliff a short distance away. He found a narrow defile that led up into the rock; followed it, and reached a little cave. There, fumbling, he at last found the electro-pistol he had hidden beneath a pile of rocks. He hurried back to the spacer and pondered what to do; he had planned no further than this. Obviously, the only thing to do was await the return of the owner: the Martian, Tarnuff, he sincerely hoped. Ron settled down comfortably beneath the rear lateral fin to wait.

It must have been hours later. Ron was aware he had dozed several times. But now he heard footsteps approaching, and he jerked himself alert. Silently he crept beneath the under curve of the hull toward the main side portal. There he stood very still in the deeper darkness and watched a lone figure approaching. It was a Martian all right, he could tell that by the huge, vague bulk of him. Ron waited until he came within a few yards—then he stepped out and said:

"Hello, Tarnuff."

The Martian stopped suddenly; then leaned forward, peering through the dark.

"An Earthman," he rasped. "What are you doing around my ship? Clear out of here!" He started to stride forward again, purposefully.

"Don't come any closer!" Jordan snapped. "I've got a pistol trained right on you."

The Martian looked down and saw it. He said tersely:

"How do you know my name? What do you want?"

Jordan didn't answer the first question, but smiled at the confirmation. "I want three things, Tarnuff. First I want you to toss your pistol over here on the ground. Next I want you to enter this ship ahead of me. Finally I want you to sign a paper. After which I may or may not let you go, depending on how you comply."

Tarnuff didn't move. He stood there staring.

"Quick—your pistol!" Jordan snapped. "Or you get a taste of mine!"

"Oh, no." Tarnuff was looking above Jordan's head. He went on quickly: "All right, Oruk, grab him!"

Jordan laughed aloud. "That old trick! I don't fall—"

His voice was cut off as two huge hands reached down and closed around his throat. At the same instant Tarnuff leaped forward and knocked the pistol from his hand.

"That old trick, eh? But sometimes it works. Nice going, Oruk."

"Heard voices—came to see," a gruff voice said.

Jordan was dangling, his toes barely touching the ground. He couldn't breathe. The hands tightened still more, as very powerful arms hauled him up into the airlock. There the hands loosened, and Jordan crumpled to the floor, half conscious. He was barely aware of Tarnuff climbing in, and his voice saying:

"Throw him in one of the empty cabins, Oruk, then stand by in the rocket room. We're taking off. I'll attend to the brave Earthman later."

---

Ron came back to full consciousness, his head spinning dizzily as the blood rushed back. He was lying on the floor of a bare metal room. The door was locked, as expected. Were they in space already? He hadn't heard the throb of the rockets. He rushed to the port and looked out. No, they were still resting in the dark hollow of Ceres. He tried the port, and to his surprise it swung open. That meant they'd be rising very soon, else Oruk wouldn't have been so careless.

Ron estimated his chances, and made up his mind quickly. He'd have to get out of here while he could, then find another entrance whereby he could gain the control room where Tarnuff was. At least the element of surprise would be in his favor. He clambered through the port and slid down the smooth curve of the ship, finally dropping to the ground ten feet below.

There were four airlocks, one pair amidships and the other pair near the prow. He tried them all. All were tightly sealed. He ran back toward the stern, looking up at the row of ports. But there were no handholds for him there, even if he could have leaped up and reached them. He stopped suddenly at the huge, rectangular under-hull repulsion plates. No, there was no entrance that way. Even as he looked at them, he heard their low steady hum begin; the entire hull began quivering. He ran on, and reached the rear fin just as the ship began to lift. With a little prayer he leaped and pulled himself up.

It was a foolhardy thing to do, Ron knew that, even as he was climbing atop a six-foot tube by using the smaller tubes as a ladder. He knew the atmosphere ended about a half-mile up; he also knew that if those tubes started blasting suddenly he'd be a cinder in no time at all.

He gained his precarious perch, and moved along toward the rocket-room port a dozen feet ahead of him. Luckily the spacer was lifting slowly. He reached the port and peered in. Oruk, a huge Jovian brute, was facing half away from Ron; his hands were on the fuel levers as though awaiting orders from Tarnuff.

The spacer stopped rising, just clear of the cliffs. The air was tenuous, barely breathable now. With frantic fingers Ron tugged at the rim around the heavy glass port. It was useless. At the same instant he saw Oruk throw several levers. The small tubes on which Ron was standing began to vibrate, and he could feel increasing heat through his heavy shoes.

Desperately he raised one foot and crashed his heel against the glass. It rang hollowly, but didn't break. Oruk turned at the sound, a startled look on his huge stupid face. Again Ron lashed out, and a third time. The glass crashed inward just as Oruk advanced toward him with powerful long arms reaching out.

The heat under Ron's feet was unbearable now. Heedless of the ragged glass, he grabbed the upper edge of the port and launched his entire body through, feet first. His feet caught the advancing Oruk squarely in the chest and sent him staggering back. Ron himself crashed to the floor.

He arose just as Oruk came at him again with slow deliberateness. Ron glanced hurriedly around for a weapon, but there was nothing. He ducked under the reaching arms, crashed a blow to the Jovian's body and another to his face. He saw Oruk grin. He tried to escape the arms, but they found him and closed around him crushingly. Ron struggled, but his own arms were pressed tight in that relentless grip. He could only stare up into the grayish face that was still grinning. The breath was slowly leaving him, the pressure on his lungs agonizing. He brought his knee up sharply into Oruk's side, but couldn't reach it. Suddenly Tarnuff's voice came through the communicating tube:

"All right, Oruk, full power now. All tubes!"

The pressure of Oruk's arms loosened for a moment as he stared around. At the same time Ron feigned unconsciousness. His head dropped forward, and he allowed his whole body to go limp. Oruk dropped him to the floor and turned to the tube.

Instantly Ron was on his feet, but silently. One leap brought him to Oruk's side, and he snatched out the pistol. Even as the Jovian was turning, Ron pressed it hard against his side and released the trigger.

It wasn't an electro-gun, it was one of the Martian-style pistols that fired tiny atomic bullets. The bullet entered Oruk's side and exploded at once, tearing a gaping hole through him. He staggered forward, his mouth open ludicrously as though he would speak; only a gurgling sound emerged, then he crashed to the floor.

---

Ron wasted a moment to lean weakly against the wall. Suddenly he saw that the ship was rising again, the air of this room swiftly escaping through the shattered port. Tarnuff was calling:

"Oruk! I said full power!"

Ron leaped to an iron locker, wrenched it open and saw a pair of space-suits. Quickly he donned one, and clamped the helmet down just as the utter cold of space swept into the room. He pressed the oxygen-tank release and breathed gratefully as air came flowing into the helmet. Then he stepped to the bank of fuel levers and pulled them all down. The spacer leaped forward, leaving Ceres far behind as triple blasts of fire streamed from the huge tubes.

Pulling Oruk's huge body after him, Ron stepped quickly into the interior of the ship and stood a moment, listening. Not a sound came from Tarnuff, far forward in the control room. Ron dragged Oruk's body to the central airlock, and gave it a decent burial in space. Not until then did he divest himself of the cumbersome space-suit. He examined the atom pistol and saw there were still five or six charges in the firing chamber. Then he moved forward, opened the control room door silently and stood just within the threshold.

Tarnuff was hunched over the calculation table, his back to the door. Once or twice he reached out and moved a directional-finder infinitesimally to agree with the chart. Ron watched silently, a grim smile on his lips. Not until Tarnuff straightened up from his task did Ron speak:

"For the second time, Tarnuff—hello."

The Martian whirled around in the seat, saw Ron with the pistol levelled.

"You!" he exclaimed, starting to spring up but sinking down again. "So—you broke out, eh? That clumsy fool, Oruk, wait'll I get my hands on him." His face darkened.

Ron laughed aloud. "You'll have a hard time doing that. Your strong-arm pal is a thousand miles behind us in space by this time. Yes," he answered the other's questioning eyes, "I blasted a hole through him." He gestured to the Martian's belt. "I'll take that pistol now; I asked for it a little while ago, you remember. First stand up, then toss it to me—careful!"

Tarnuff obeyed, sullenly. Ron caught the pistol and jammed it in his belt.

"And now my electro-gun, please. That's right. Thanks. You've got your course charted?"

"Yes."

"For where?"

"Callisto."

"Good enough for the time being. Now lock those controls and sit down at the table again. We'll get down to business."

"I haven't any business with you, Earthman."

"Oh, yes you have, but you don't know it yet. Sit down!" Ron shoved the pistol at him meaningly.

Tarnuff complied, appearing more puzzled than he was sullen. But he did not remain puzzled long, as Ron drew out a folded paper and handed it to him.

"I'm Ron Jordan. The name may mean something to you when you've read that. You will then sign it, if you wish to ever leave this ship alive."

Ron watched him closely as he read, and he saw comprehension slowly dawn in the Martian's eyes. Tarnuff finished the brief, but concise story of the asteroid incident as related by Carl Jordan. Then he looked up with an almost contemptuous smile on his lips.

"Ah, yes, I remember now. Your brother, I presume. I had heard on the telecast that he was sentenced for smuggling Silicytes. Most unfortunate."

"Unfortunate for you, right now. Sign!"

Tarnuff calmly ignored the menacing pistol and said:

"But this statement implicates me most seriously, Ron Jordan. I do not like that."

"Sign," Ron said through clenched teeth, "or I blast you here and now."

Tarnuff shook his head. "That's one thing I know you won't do. Not without my signature. You need it too badly."

"Do I? You forget one thing, Tarnuff. The Patrol's still looking for a ship named *Lucifer* and your attempt to disguise it was pretty clumsy. I had intended to let you escape at your convenience, but now I'll just have to take you *and* this ship back to Earth. That should be conclusive enough."

But Tarnuff was smiling blandly, leaning back in the chair. He was hugely amused at something, and Ron was vaguely worried without exactly knowing why.

"No, Ron Jordan," the Martian was saying. "I don't think you'll dare set this spacer on Earth or any other planet."

"Why not?"

"Because you know too well the penalty for Silicyte smuggling. Has it not occurred to you what my cargo is? I'm carrying a full load of Silicytes at this moment. As soon as you set down anywhere I'll swear to the authorities that you're my accomplice in this. They'll believe it, too, in view of what happened to your brother; they'll think slave trading runs in your family!" Tarnuff laughed harshly, looking up at Ron's suddenly perplexed face.

---

It was several seconds before Ron could realize the implication of the words. Then he said explosively:

"I don't believe you!"

"You don't believe I've got the Silicytes aboard? Come and see for yourself."

Ron knew by the man's cool insolence that he spoke the truth. But he followed Tarnuff back into the ship anyway, keeping him at pistol point. The Martian unlocked and threw back several doors ... and there were the Silicytes. Only twice in his life had Ron ever seen the queer creatures, and never at this close range.

They stood erect, and were roughly human in shape, but that's as far as the resemblance went. They were formed of thousands of faceted crystals which clung together with peculiar cohesion, flashing iridescently whenever they moved! Instead of arms, dozens of chain-like crystalline tentacles hung down from a position near the shoulders. The creatures appeared so brittle and fragile that it seemed they would fall apart at the slightest touch, but this was purely illusion. They possessed a dull sort of intelligence but obeyed instructions implicitly once they understood, and they'd work for tremendous lengths of time to earn the scraps of metal which they absorbed and relished. For this reason they brought fabulous prices on such outposts as Callisto, despite the fact that the owners had to work them discreetly, hiding them whenever inspectors came.

"You see, Jordan?" Tarnuff said, closing the doors. "And that's only part of 'em. I've got over a hundred aboard. You can put the pistol away now, you won't need it." He moved past Ron and back to the control room.

Ron followed him slowly, pondering the unexpected and hazardous situation he found himself in. Hazardous because the Patrol had a special contingent in the asteroid lanes in an effort to stop the Silicyte smuggling which had reached unprecedented heights in the past year. Tarnuff was right—he dared not take this ship back to Earth now; and if a Patrol ship intercepted them in space, he'd soon be keeping Carl company in the Venus prison-swamp.

No he wouldn't, either! Worse than that. Caught red-handed with Silicytes in transit would mean the death penalty.

"Well, it's your move, Jordan." The Martian's voice, his entire mien, was one of amused complacency. He stepped to the controls. "Shall I re-chart for Earth?"

"No!" The word came explosively, and Ron was immediately sorry.

Tarnuff chuckled. "I thought not. Well?"

"We keep on for Callisto," Ron said with a finality he didn't feel. "It's nearer."

Tarnuff was still unperturbed. "Oh, I see. And there you turn me over to the authorities, eh? Well, Jordan, that means you cut your own throat; I meant it what I said; you're in this with me now."

Ron stood motionless, frowning and indecisive.

Tarnuff's voice was suddenly serious. "Come, Jordan, you're in a spot and you know it. So am I—I want to get these Silicytes through safely. So I'll make you a proposition. Come in this with me! I know how to land these things on Callisto and how to get rid of 'em. We'll have the cash an hour after we land there. This *was* to be my last load—it's getting risky—but I know where I can get a hundred more, and with your help we can get them through too. We'll split fifty-fifty."

Ron smiled thinly, indicating the pistols in his belt. "You're in a hell of a position to be talking like that, Tarnuff. If I wanted the Silicytes I'd take 'em all. But I don't want any part of your filthy business!"

The smile on the Martian's leathery face faded into a dark frown. "Oh. Just like your brother, eh? All right, about this time tomorrow we'll be approaching Callisto, and what then? Maybe you'll be joining your brother. I've heard that the Venus swamp is a slow and hideous death. Some men prefer the swiftness of the Ray-chamber to it...."

Ron knew that, and involuntarily he winced. He had come out here to clear Carl, he had waited a long weary month for the opportunity, and then he had bungled it.

Tarnuff pressed his advantage.

"Since you have a peculiar aversion to breaking the Earth-made laws, I can think of only one other way out of our little stalemate. A way which I, personally, prefer. But I wonder if you would dare?"

Ron looked at Tarnuff narrowly, and didn't like the smile which had appeared again on his face; there was a mocking challenge in it. Tarnuff went on:

"I would much prefer, in your Earth idiom, to comb you out of my hair and continue unhampered to Callisto. But as matters stand"—he glanced shrewdly at Ron's hand, which hovered near the weapons in his belt—"you have control of this ship at the present moment. On the other hand you need my signature on this statement to clear your brother of his sentence. True, the statement implicates me to the fullest extent of the law...."

He paused, the smile on his face widened imperceptibly, and Ron nodded impatient agreement.

"Nevertheless," Tarnuff went on, "I will sign this damnatory statement."

Ron stepped forward eagerly. "You will? Good. Now you're talking."

"On one condition."

"No conditions!"

"I will sign this paper," the Martian went on, "and I will keep it in my possession. My conditions are that if I give you a chance at it, you'll give me an equal chance to take over this ship again. In other words—one of us takes everything."

Ron frowned. "What are you driving at?"

"Exactly this. I intend that if this ship reaches Callisto, I'll be the only man alive on it. On the other hand it may reach Earth; if it does, *you'll* be the only man alive on it, and you'll have my signed statement clearing both yourself and your brother."

Ron was listening. "Go on," he said.

Tarnuff indicated the pistols in Ron's belt. "Two identical atom pistols there. The Martian *V'Nith*—you have heard of it?"

---

Ron was suddenly tense, standing there; his brain was spinning with the idea. Yes, he had heard of it—the cunning dueling game which men like Tarnuff sometimes engaged in, mostly on the dark asteroids; the duel which called for the most infinite precision and cunning; in which the first mistake usually meant death.

Tarnuff was watching Ron shrewdly now; he saw his indecision; he said sharply:

"All or nothing, man! Get it over with quickly! After all, you've more to gain than I ... your brother's life and your own."

"Also more to lose," Ron muttered. He glanced around the control cabin. "But here, in the ship? How—"

"No, of course not here! One loose atomic bullet would blast through the hull. We combat outside, and only one of us will enter this ship again."

Ron drew one of the Martian pistols, hoisted it thoughtfully in his hand. He had slain Oruk with it. That had been the first time he'd ever fired one. But he liked the easy, comfortable feel, every bit as familiar as his own electro-pistol.

"Well?" Tarnuff was impatient.

With a sudden surge of confidence Ron made up his mind.

"You're right, Tarnuff. We'll get it over with one way or the other! I think I'm as good a man as you at any game! Rules?"

Tarnuff, smiling, held up one finger. "One apiece."

"You're going to make it precise, eh? That's okay by me. I'm considered a pretty good shot with any kind of pistol."

"And I," replied Tarnuff with easy arrogance, "have killed four men on the asteroids in duels such as this. Marksmanship is not all."

Ron nodded. He removed the charges from both firing chambers, making very sure that only one charge was left in each.

"Your electro-pistol," Tarnuff said. "Leave it here in the control room. Not that I don't trust you, but everything must be equal."

"I've a better idea than that. I don't trust you either. Want to watch this?" Ron donned a space-suit again, stepped into the airlock and hurled his electro-pistol far away into the void where it drifted out of reach forever. Tarnuff, watching from a port, nodded his satisfaction as Ron returned.

"And now the statement," Ron said, drawing the paper from his pocket. "Which you will sign, after first adding a P.S. absolving *me* entirely if I should be apprehended with these Silicytes on my hands."

Tarnuff looked up, smiling. "You think of everything, don't you?"

"It pays."

Tarnuff wrote for a minute, signed, and handed it to Ron. The latter read it and was satisfied.

Tarnuff took the paper from Ron's hands again and slipped it into his own pocket. "If I win I shall destroy this. If you win, which I doubt, you may take it from me at your convenience."

"You think of everything too. Okay," Ron shrugged. He held out the identical pistols. "Your choice, if it means anything."

"It doesn't, but I'll take this one." Tarnuff took one of the pistols and then climbed into a space-suit as Ron waited.

"Which airlocks?" Ron asked through the audio-phone in his helmet.

"I'd suggest the central ones. I'll take the port side and you the starboard. We'll enter the respective locks at the same instant, then into space. After that, well, only one of us will enter this ship again."

They moved into parallel corridors on opposite sides of the ship. Instantly Ron was alert, not trusting the Martian out of his sight now that they were both armed with a bullet apiece. But both their helmet phones were on. Ron stopped a moment and listened. He heard the other's amused voice:

"Stopping, Jordan? On to your airlock! Goodbye, but don't mind if I don't wish you good luck!"

"The same to you." Ron entered his lock. The inner door closed automatically, and a few seconds later the outer door opened. He knew Tarnuff had done likewise, for he could hear the faint sound of the mechanism through his phones. Then he knew that Tarnuff had swung outside, for he heard a couple of metallic clicks as the magnetic shoes made contact on the outer, opposite side of the hull.

Satisfied, Ron moved out too, and his own shoes swung around in an arc to make contact.

---

For a single instant he was appalled at the utter, outer immensity, the sweeping darkness; then he did not look outward again, but clung to the hull, facing it. He knew the *Lucifer* was still speeding along on its full rocket blast, but not relative to him.

The helmet phones had given him an idea. He held his breath, listening. He heard the faint clicks of Tarnuff's shoes as he moved along on the opposite side. He seemed to be moving toward the bow. Then Ron heard a different click, as Tarnuff shut off his phone. Ron chuckled as he reached up and shut off his own. He was sure Tarnuff had done that deliberately, and probably was reversing his direction and moving sternward now.

Ron didn't move at all for a minute. He clung there lightly, peering up along the sweeping curve of the hull above his head, ready to use his pistol if Tarnuff should appear there. But Tarnuff didn't appear, and Ron thought it likely he wouldn't for awhile. He hadn't forgotten the other's words, "marksmanship is not all." One bullet apiece! Probably Tarnuff would try to make him waste his bullet, thus putting Ron at his mercy. That would be the logical thing to do.

Keeping this in mind, Ron moved carefully sternward. He held the pistol ready in his hand. Occasionally he peered upward along the curve, alert and ready for anything. He wondered what Tarnuff had in mind. But this wasn't a guessing game, it was far more deadly than that, and he'd have to be very sure before he fired his bullet.

But there was still another danger. This hull was his only world now and he was almost weightless. He clung to it fiercely as he inched along, knowing that it wouldn't take much of a shove to send him drifting free, out of its gravity forever. He looked along the straight line of it and saw the faint glow of the rocket blasts. His brain writhed at a sudden horrible thought. Would Tarnuff try to gain the control room again, change the course suddenly and thus shake him off into space?

At this thought Ron hurried his progress a little, making for the four parallel side tubes he could see a little distance away. They were the only tubes that weren't blasting, being used only in emergency; they would allow him firmer footage, and maybe it would be a good idea to wait there until Tarnuff came somewhere in sight.

As he neared these tubes, something seemed wrong with them. There was something else there—a vague dark blur—between the second and third tubes. Ron stopped suddenly. Could Tarnuff have reached there already? No, that was impossible. He moved forward cautiously, and the blur didn't stir.

And then Ron saw what it was. And he was glad he had shut off his helmet phone, for he laughed loudly, a little hysterically, the sound almost bursting his ear-drums inside the helmet.

Wedged between those horizontally parallel tubes was Oruk's huge body which Ron had thought he had buried in space! Apparently it had been caught in the gravity of the ship again, and had slid slowly along the hull, luckily right in line with those tubes, to finally come to rest there.

Ron had been indecisive. Now he felt his brain become suddenly cool and concise. He knew what he must do. It had been pure luck that *he* had taken the starboard side instead of Tarnuff. It was an omen.

But it would be risky. Ron suddenly sobered, moved along until he could grasp Oruk by the collar. He tugged. The body was wedged tight, just fitting the space between the tubes. Ron thrust the pistol into his belt and used both hands. At last the body came free.

He saw that he'd have to leave the pistol in his belt now. If Tarnuff should suddenly appear somewhere over the curve of the hull, it would be the end. But he'd have to risk it.

Hugging the body tightly to him, he moved a little higher, up to the long line of circular ports. He moved slowly back toward the center of the ship, peering into each glassite port as he passed. But he couldn't find what he was looking for; all was dark within.

At last he came to one that wasn't so dark. He saw a faint scintillation of color. Silicytes! There were at least a score of them in this cabin into which he peered. He had almost forgotten about them, but now he was glad of their faint flashing light, for he saw what he sought: one of the lockers containing space-suits.

He knew the Silicytes could live in airless space, so he didn't hesitate. A few blows with his metallic shoe, and the port shattered.

It was almost his undoing. The rush of air from the room came so suddenly it almost swept him away into space. Just in time he grasped the edge of the circular opening with one hand, clung tenaciously to his gruesome burden with the other. Then the air was gone, and he shoved Oruk's body into the room ahead of him.

Instantly the Silicytes crowded around, their chain-like tentacles clashing, reaching out toward him. Ron could feel their crystal coldness even through his space-suit. He shoved them recklessly out of the way, knowing they were harmless. At last he procured a space-suit, and then came a job not to his liking—fitting Oruk's huge body into it. At last, however, it was accomplished. He shoved the bulging, helmeted figure outside again, and climbed out beside it.

Ron's lips tightened grimly now. If his luck held, he'd make Tarnuff waste his bullet....

But where was Tarnuff? For a second Ron thought of clicking on his phone again and calling out, to see what would happen. But no—that would give his own position away. If he didn't know where Tarnuff was, neither did the Martian know where he was.

Ron took a guess and moved toward the stern again.

He knew he would have to be doubly careful now, and yet paradoxically he'd have to take a chance. With difficulty he held the space-suited figure close to his side. As he came ever nearer the stern he began to move oblique upward, peering intently all along the hull's horizon for a sight of Tarnuff. Would this trick work? Perhaps Tarnuff wouldn't fire at the first sight of a space-helmeted figure, as Ron hoped. And yet—why not? He'd be expecting no other moving figure out there except Ron's.

Ron was almost at the stern tubes now. He began to wonder if Tarnuff had taken the other direction after all, toward the bow off the ship. He took a firmer hold on the body beside him, moved a few more feet obliquely upward, and then ... he had guessed right! He saw the Martian!

Ron caught only a glimpse of him, flattened against the hull with his pistol held ready, before he jerked his own head down again. He looked at Oruk's dead grayish face inside the plate so close to his own. He could only hope that Tarnuff wouldn't recognize it. Luckily the two helmets were identical, and Ron was sure that if Tarnuff fired at all, it would be at the face-plate.

It was a gruesome thing to do, but this was no time for squeamishness, Ron thought, as he began easing the body up inches at a time. It was the age-old trick to draw the enemys fire.

Nothing happened. He pushed the body higher, almost recklessly, but maintained a firm grip on it. Still higher. He was sure it must be at least partially in Tarnuff's line of vision by now. Why didn't he fire? Could he have detected—

And then it did happen, so suddenly that Ron couldn't even gasp his surprise. There was an abrupt puff of atomic dust above him; at the same instant he felt Oruk's body torn spinning out of his grasp. Then he saw the space-suited figure drifting lazily outward. It was grotesque, headless.

The ruse had worked! Tarnuff had fired his bullet, and very accurately! Ron felt a fierce surge of exultation as he drew his own pistol and then hauled himself swiftly up into Tarnuff's sight.

Tarnuff had risen to his feet. He still held the pistol loosely in his hand. A satisfied little smile was on his lips. Then he caught sight of Ron, the smile vanished, the pistol fell and went skidding lightly across the hull. The expression on his face was so ludicrous that Ron wanted to laugh. Instead, he reached up and clicked on his helmet phone, motioning Tarnuff to do the same.

"Beat you!" Ron cried fiercely. "Beat you at your own game, Tarnuff, and it was easy! Now, before I kill you, I want you to know it's going to be the greatest pleasure of my life!"

Tarnuff looked out at the drifting body he had just blasted. He nodded, and when he spoke his voice almost purred.

"Ah, now I see. Clever, Jordan, very clever. But don't congratulate yourself too soon, because you haven't won yet! We're back at the stalemate again. Why don't you pull the trigger, Jordan? Go ahead and pull it—and blast yourself to dust!"

Startled, Ron looked down at the weapon in his hand. Now it was Tarnuff who was exultant as he went on:

"You never had a chance, Jordan! Never from the beginning! You see, I counted on your Earth chivalry, and you did just what I expected—gave me my choice of what you thought were identical pistols. But they aren't identical! The one you now hold works in reverse! Such reverse pistols have stood me in good stead on several occasions, and I always make it a point to have one with me. Fire it—and you blast yourself, not me!"

---

They stood facing each other, perhaps thirty feet apart. Tarnuff glanced down and saw the pistol he had dropped. He reached out with his foot and slid it along the hull to Jordan.

"There you are. If you'll compare the two, you'll see that the firing mechanism of yours is in reverse. One needs to look very closely to detect the difference."

Ron didn't bother to pick up the weapon.

"You know I don't know a thing about these Martian pistols, Tarnuff."

"Exactly. You don't."

Ron glanced at the gun in his hand, keeping a wary eye on Tarnuff. The strange weapon looked all right to him—and yet even his inexperienced eye saw that it *might* very easily have been tampered with so that the atomic bullet would explode in the chamber. He did know that these were dangerous and tricky weapons, and that's why most men preferred the Earth electro-pistols.

"All right, Tarnuff, we'll settle it without weapons! I—"

Ron stopped suddenly. Something was wrong with Tarnuff. The Martian was staring past him, real horror on his face and in his voice as he whispered hoarsely:

"My God ... Jordan!"

Ron knew this was no trick. Tarnuff was terrified.

Ron whirled, stared—and became frozen. The pistol, Tarnuff, everything else was forgotten as he felt a chill go up his spine at the sight.

Literally dozens of Silicytes were swarming all over the hull amidships ... and they seemed to be absorbing the metal, literally devouring it, digesting it! Already a gaping hole was in the hull, and it grew even larger as more Silicytes came swarming up from below, to join in the fantastic meal!

"You did this!" Tarnuff was shrieking now at Ron. "You fool, you must have let them out one of the portholes! I had those rooms lined with wood, the one thing they won't digest—and you let them escape!"

Ron paid little heed to Tarnuff's raging, but went leaping toward the Silicytes, with some notion of throwing them off into space, anything to get them away from there. But he couldn't even reach them. When he was yet yards away, he felt a fierce heat exuding from them, heat generated by the digested metal! And he saw them becoming slowly, rosy radiant.

The heat drove Ron away. He turned and walked back toward Tarnuff again. The latter hadn't moved.

"Well, Jordan," he grated, "I hope you're satisfied with your bungling! Here goes the *Lucifer* right from under us, thanks to you. There's enough oxygen in these space-suits for about one more hour."

"Well, I wouldn't worry about it!" Ron laughed suddenly, laughed in joyous relief, and pointed. "Look! Here comes help, and just in the neck of time!"

Far behind them a tiny silvery dot was barely discernible against the darkness; but it grew steadily larger as it took on the shape of a space-ship, moving unmistakably toward them. They watched in silence as it came nearer.

Suddenly Tarnuff exclaimed:

"Help, did you say, Jordan? Here comes the final touch, you mean—our finish! That's a patroller!"

"Are you sure of that, Tarnuff?"

"Sure of it? Man, I've been dodging the Patrol so much out here that I can tell 'em a million miles off!"

"So—I win after all, Tarnuff! That statement you signed absolves me. Let 'em come!" Ron waved his arms wildly in the direction of the approaching ship. "Come on you birds, step on it!"

Tarnuff reached suddenly in his pocket and brought out the folded paper.

"Yes, it does clear you, doesn't it? You and your brother both! Thanks for reminding me, Jordan, in the excitement I almost forgot about that...."

And then Tarnuff's voice became shrill with maniac glee:

"But it won't do either of you any good! By the time that Patrol ship gets here there won't be any paper!"

He whirled suddenly and leaped toward the stern rocket tubes only a few yards away.

In a flash of horror Ron realized his intention—to destroy that paper in the rocket blast! Ron took two bounding steps after him, and then realized he could never catch him in time. But Ron still held the atom pistol. He swung his arm stiffly up in a straight line with Tarnuff's back, and pulled the trigger.

It was a purely instinctive action, and not until a split second later did Ron realize it. And he laughed wildly then, for Tarnuff *had* been bluffing about that pistol; there was no reverse action to it. He saw the center of Tarnuff's back explode in ghastly devastation. Then Tarnuff, or what was left of him, plunged head foremost down along the sharp curve of the hull toward the rocket tubes.

Ron leaped after him, but it was too late. He saw the crumpled paper jarred from Tarnuff's outflung hand. It drifted lazily on, down over the rocket tube and then out into the blast, where it vanished in an insignificant little puff of flame.

Ron was suddenly very weary. He didn't move from where he stood, he just sat down there, bowed his head in his hands, and waited.

---

"Hello, hello. Jordan, is it? Can you hear us? Hello!" The voice came so faintly in Ron's ears that it sounded like a dream. He lifted his head, stared around, and then realized it was coming through his phone.

"Yeah, I hear you," he replied tonelessly, looking out at the Patrol ship which was nearer than he had supposed.

"Commander Graham of Patrol ship *Terra* speaking! Lucky thing for you, Jordan—we've had you in our magniview plate for the past half-hour, and in our phones for the past ten minutes. We heard everything, so don't worry, you're in the clear. That *is* the *Lucifer* I suppose?"

"You suppose right, Commander! Come and get it!"

Ron looked back at the Silicytes. They were still at it! The damn things were insatiable! The gaping hole had widened perceptibly, and they were working in his direction now. Ron could almost imagine he felt the heat of them already.

He leaped to his feet and turned on his helmet phone full power.

"Hey, Commander!" he yelled. "Pardon me for asking, but how long would it take you to hurry? You'd better get here in five minutes or I'll be a mere hunk of dessert for these animated rock-piles. Step on those rockets!"

He heard someone chuckling, and then he sighed his relief as he saw the Patroller respond with full blast.

---

[1] Entities of silicon found only on the large asteroids. Almost human in shape and actions, they possess a silicic life-base rather than carbon, and remain a puzzle to scientists who have studied them. Being comparatively docile, reasonably intelligent, and tireless workers, they were originally brought to Earth for purposes of cheap labor. It was soon discovered, however, that they could be very dangerous. They possessed a fantastic and insatiable appetite for *metal*, and if not closely watched would destroy any with which they came in contact—first corroding it by means of peculiar crystalline emanations, and then digesting it. After some very calamitous experiences, the law was passed in 2139 forbidding any Silicytes being removed from the asteroids, on penalty of death.